Norma Snows

Paula Metcalf

Macmillan Children's Books

For Chez

First published 2008 by Macmillan Children's Books
a division of Macmillan Publishers Limited
20 New Wharf Road, London N1 9RR
Basingstoke and Oxford
Associated companies throughout the world
www.panmacmillan.com

ISBN: 978-0-230-53177-2

Text and illustrations copyright © Paula Metcalf 2008
Moral rights asserted.

3 5 7 9 8 6 4

A CIP catalogue record for this book is available from the British Library.

Printed in Belgium by Proost

Mr and Mrs Snows looked proudly at their beautiful, brand new daughter.

"Let's call her Norma," said Mr Snows.

"Norma Snows suits her perfectly!" said Mrs Snows.

At the local Parent and Toddler group, Mrs Snows was the envy of all the other mums and dads.

What they would have given for a hands-free baby!

Norma was the first baby to learn how to crawl.

Mrs Snows was very proud.

As she got older, Norma became a very helpful girl.

She helped with the shopping . . .

she helped with
the laundry . . .

and she helped keep Dad
out of her mum's hair.

When she started school, it became clear that
Norma was not only helpful but talented too.

Music lessons were her favourite.

She was brilliant at gymnastics!

And on Sports
Day, Norma won
the running,
hopping AND
skipping races . . .

by a nose.

One morning, Norma was practising her hula-hooping skills in the playground.

"Is there no end to your talents?" her teacher asked.

"I don't think so," replied Norma.

But then she started to worry. What if she did run out of talents?

Later on, Norma's class were learning about aeroplanes, but Norma wasn't listening. She was too busy thinking . . .

"Aeroplanes have long noses which help them to glide through the sky," the teacher was saying.

Suddenly Norma's ears pricked up.

Just like me, she thought.

That lunchtime, Norma wrote an exciting message on the board.

When lessons had finished, Norma
led everyone out to the field.

"Please keep off the runway!" shouted Norma.
"Whoops! I mean run up!"

Eyes set on the sky, Norma started to run.
Faster and faster, she raced down the field.

Finally, with a huge leap . . .

She took off. Up and up she went . . .

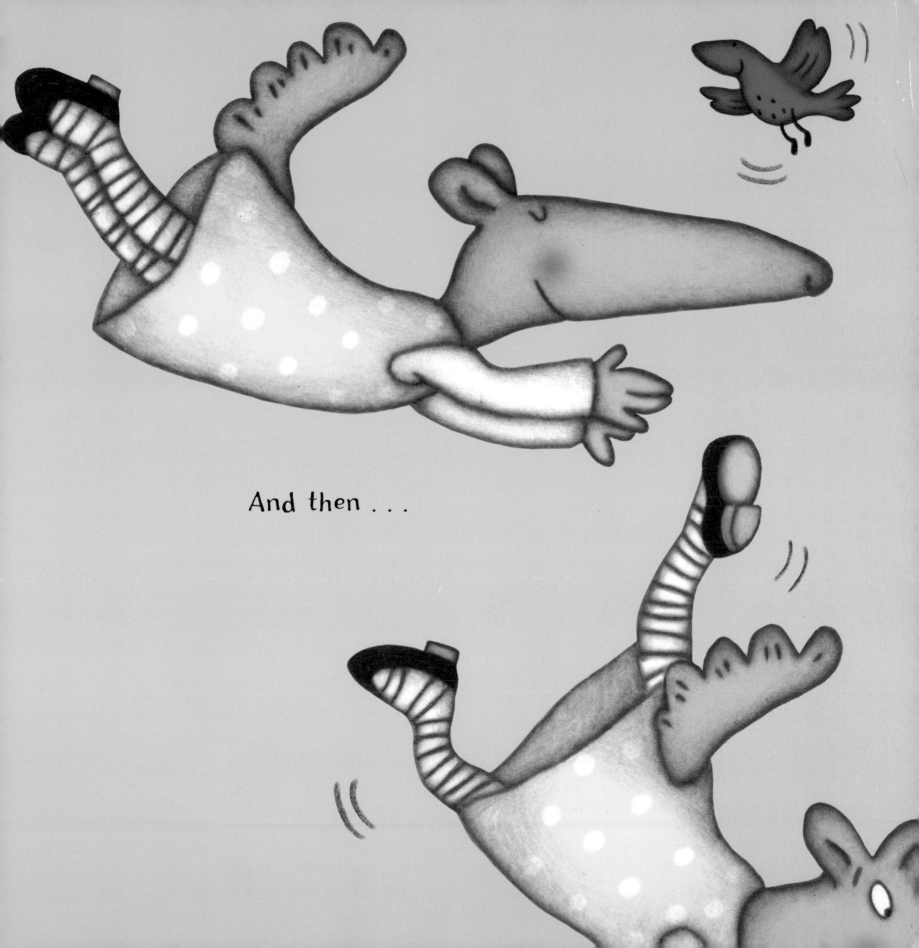

And then . . .

Suddenly, everything went black.

When Norma opened her eyes, the world looked very different.

"Oh dear!" gasped the teacher.
"Are you OK?"

For a few moments Norma stared at her audience in silence. Then, very slowly, a big upside-down smile spread across her face.

"Of course I'm OK!" she giggled. "That went perfectly! Behold the world's first ever . . .

"NO-HANDED

HANDSTAND!"

Norma breathed a sigh
of relief. It seemed there
was no end to her
talents after all!